A Note to Parents

For many children, learning math is difficult and "I hate math!" is their first response — to which many parents silently add "Me, too!" Children often see adults comfortably reading and writing, but they rarely have such models for mathematics. And math fear can be catching!

The easy-to-read stories in this **Hello Reader! Math** series were written to give children a positive introduction to mathematics, and parents a pleasurable re-acquaintance with a subject that is important to everyone's life. **Hello Reader! Math** stories make mathematical ideas accessible, interesting, and fun for children. The activities and suggestions at the end of each book provide parents with a hands-on approach to help children develop mathematical interest and confidence.

Enjoy the mathematics!

• Give your child a chance to retell the story. The more familiar children are with the story, the more they will understand its mathematical concepts.
• Use the colorful illustrations to help children "hear and see" the math at work in the story.
• Treat the math activities as games to be played for fun. Follow your child's lead. Spend time on those activities that engage your child's interest and curiosity.
• Activities, especially ones using physical materials, help make abstract mathematical ideas concrete.

Learning is a messy process. Learning about math calls for children to become immersed in lively experiences that help them make sense of mathematical concepts and symbols.

Although learning about numbers is basic to math, other ideas, such as identifying shapes and patterns, measuring, collecting and interpreting data, reasoning logically, and thinking about chance, are also important. By reading these stories and having fun with the activities, you will help your child enthusiastically say "**Hello, math**," instead of "I hate math."

—Marilyn Burns
National Mathematics Educator
Author of *The I Hate Mathematics! Book*

For the memory of Grandma Adele
— J.R.

For Niki, a great math teacher
— C.P.

Copyright © 2000 by Scholastic Inc.
The activities on pages 43-48 copyright © 2000 by Marilyn Burns.
All rights reserved. Published by Scholastic Inc.
SCHOLASTIC, HELLO READER!, CARTWHEEL BOOKS and associated logos are trademarks and/or registered trademarks of Scholastic Inc.

Library of Congress Cataloging-in-Publication Data
Rocklin, Joanne.
    The incredibly awesome box / by Joanne Rocklin; illustrated by Cary Pillo; math activities by Marilyn Burns.
        p.   cm.— (Hello reader! Math. Level 3)
        Summary: Jan sends her friend Nick e-mail messages describing how she and her cousins learn about shapes as they try to assemble a present for their grandmother's birthday. Includes related activities.
        ISBN 0-439-09955-2
        [1. Shape— Fiction.   2. Gifts— Fiction   Computers— Fiction.]   I. Pillo,Cary, ill.
    II. Burns, Marilyn, 1941   III. Title.   IV. Series.

PZ7.R59 In 2000
[E]— dc21   99-033967

10 9 8 7 6 5 4 3 2 1   00 01 02 03 04
                    Printed in the U.S.A.   24
                    First printing, March 2000

THE INCREDIBLY AWESOME BOX

A STORY ABOUT 3-D SHAPES

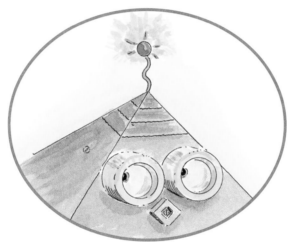

by Joanne Rocklin
Illustrated by Cary Pillo
Math Activities by Marilyn Burns

Hello Reader! Math — Level 3

SCHOLASTIC INC.

New York   Toronto   London   Auckland   Sydney   Mexico City   New Delhi   Hong Kong

Subject: A GREAT BIG MISTAKE

Dear Nick,

I miss you.

Why did you have to move so far away?

I wish you still lived here on Pine Street

because I have so much to tell you.

Wait until you hear what happened.

It was awesome!

Incredible!

Fantastic!

If I hadn't been there,

I wouldn't believe it myself.

But it's all true. Read on!

Last Saturday was Grandma Ada's
eightieth birthday.
My cousins and I were going to throw her
a big party.
Mom had already helped us order
Grandma's gift.
We didn't even have to go to a store, we
shopped through my computer. (That was
my great idea!)
We went to a web site called "Terrific Gifts"
and chose TG 124, a beautiful pen.
My four cousins and I chipped in $5.00 each.
Mom added another $10.00.

By Saturday, we were all worried —
nothing had arrived.
That morning we looked up Pine Street.
We looked down Pine Street.
"I see it!" yelled Max. "Here comes the truck!"
"At last," Kathy sighed.
"Hooray!" cheered the twins, Ed and Ellie.
"Hooray, hooray!" I shouted, louder than anyone.

"See? I told you the gift would get here on time!" I said. "You are a bunch of silly worrywarts!"

"I'm still worried, Jan," said Kathy.

"Why?" I asked.

"Look," she said.

The delivery people were carrying a big square box.

A huge box.

A GIGANTIC box.

"Who is Jan?" asked the deliverywoman.

"That's me," I said.

"Sign here," said the deliveryman.

"Somebody made a mistake," I said. "That is a very big box and we only ordered one small pen."

"If there's a problem, call Terrific Gifts," said the deliveryman.

"Here's the phone number," said the deliverywoman.

They put the big box down and hopped back into their truck.

"There must be a thousand pens
in this big box!" said Max.
"Or one giant-sized pen," I said.
That's when I saw the tag.
It said TG 123.
We had ordered TG 124!
"Wait!" I shouted.
"You delivered the wrong thing!"
But it was too late. The truck was gone.

That's all for now, Nick.
G2G—Got to Go.
I have to walk the dog.
To be continued!!!!

Your best friend,
Jan

From: JANCAN

To: COOLNICK

Subject: WHAT'S IN THE BOX?

Dear Nick,

Here I am back again.

I'll bet you can't wait to hear what happened next!

Where was I? Oh, I remember now.

Saturday. It was already noon.

Grandma's party was supposed to start at five p.m.

We dragged the huge box into my bedroom.
We sure could have used your help, Nick!

"What do you think is in here?" asked Max.

"A refrigerator," said Ellie.

"But a refrigerator is a different shape," said
Kathy. "The sides of this box are squares."

"Then maybe there are two refrigerators
inside," Ed said hopefully.

"Don't be silly," said Max.

"That would be too heavy to carry."

"How about a rabbit in a rabbit hutch?" asked Kathy.

"I don't think so," I said slowly. "I don't see any air holes to help the rabbit breathe."

"I know!" said Ed. "It's a big TV!"

"You're right!" Kathy answered. "A square TV would fit very well in this big square box."

"Grandma Ada would love a new TV," Ellie said. "Her old TV doesn't work very well."

I looked at the price tag.

"TG 123 is the same price as TG 124," I said.

"Hooray!" said Ed. "Then we can keep the new TV for Grandma."

"What sort of TV costs $35?" Max asked.

"Let's look and see," I said.

I opened the box
and looked inside.
I did not see a TV.
I did not see a rabbit or a refrigerator.
I saw different shaped blocks.
Some had curved edges.
Some had straight edges.
Some had curved sides.
Some had flat sides.
Some blocks could roll.
Some blocks could slide.
Some had lots of corners.
Some had only one.
And some had no corners at all.

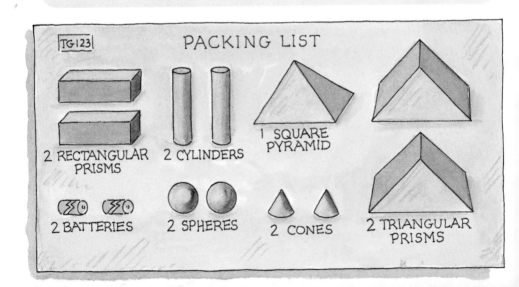

TG-123 PACKING LIST

2 RECTANGULAR PRISMS   2 CYLINDERS   1 SQUARE PYRAMID

2 BATTERIES   2 SPHERES   2 CONES   2 TRIANGULAR PRISMS

"Blocks!" shouted Ed and Ellie. "Let's build a tower!"

"Look, there's a note," I said. "THE INCREDIBLE TG 123," I read. "Batteries included."

"What's so incredible about a bunch of blocks?" asked Max.

"Blocks are a terrific gift for little kids," said Kathy. "But they're a terrible gift for a grandmother."

Something crashed. The twins cried.

Kathy was right. The TG 123 was an awful gift for Grandma Ada.

And it was all my fault!

G2G. Mom just told me to get to bed. Stay tuned until tomorrow, Nick.

Your best friend,
Jan

Dear Nick,

I have a lot of homework to do tonight,

but I wanted to e-mail you first.

My incredible, unbelievable story isn't

finished yet.

It gets even more fantastic!

Here's what happened next:

Saturday afternoon I called Terrific Gifts.

"You have reached Terrific Gifts," a voice said.

"Our hours are from nine a.m. until five p.m."

I looked at my watch. It was only 1:30 p.m.

"But we are closed on weekends," the voice

continued.

I hung up the phone.

Now what were we going to do?

I turned on my computer.

Kathy got angry.

"You can't play computer games now!" she said. "We have so much to do for Grandma Ada's birthday party!"

"I'm not playing a game," I explained. "I have an idea."

I went to the web site for Terrific Gifts.

I clicked on TG 123.

I clicked on HELP.

I clicked on BUILD THE INCREDIBLE

TG 123 IN ONLY FOUR STEPS!

"Four steps," said Kathy. "That sounds easy."

"It doesn't say four easy steps," said Max.

"You are being a worrywart again," I said.

"We can do it!"

I heard a shout: "Watch out!"

The twins were at it again.

"Step One," I read from the computer screen.

"Find two rectangular prisms.

Stand them up tall and attach a sphere on each top."

"This is too hard," said Max. "See you later.

I'm going to blow up some balloons."

Kathy, Ed, Ellie, and I didn't give up.

I clicked on SPHERE.

This is the answer we got:

"Not like a box,

Not like a book,

It is always the same

Wherever you look."

"I know!" Kathy cried.

She found the two spheres.

Now I clicked on RECTANGULAR PRISM.

"I don't get it," said Ellie.

Ed ran into the kitchen.

He brought back a stick of butter from the refrigerator.

He turned it every which way.

Ed shrugged his shoulders. Ellie shook her head.

I typed in MORE HELP.

"I still don't get it," said Ed.

"I do!" I said.

I found the two rectangular prisms.

"See?" I said. "Two edges are the same length. The other two edges are a different length. And the corners are all exactly the same."

I read step one out loud again.

Ed attached a sphere to a rectangular prism.

Then something weird happened.

The prism started glowing.

The sphere started spinning.

"Look at that!" I cried.

"Look at what?" Ed asked.

"I don't see anything," Ellie added.

I took another look at the prism with the

sphere attached.

Nothing moved.

Kathy looked at her watch.

She picked up the stick of butter.

"I am going to help Mom bake a cake for

Grandma," she said.

Now only Ed, Ellie, and I were left.

But not for long!!!

I'd like to keep writing, but Mom just told me

to get going on my homework.

To be continued!!!!

Your best friend,

Jan

From: JANCAN

To: COOLNICK

Subject: SOMETHING SILLY!

Dear Nick,

Sorry I missed your phone call today!

I called you back, but you were out.

I would have loved to have told you myself

what else happened on that surprising

Saturday.

Well, I'll just have to keep telling my story in

e-mail. Here goes:

I clicked on STEP TWO.

"Find two cylinders,"

appeared on the computer screen. "Attach a

cone to the end of each cylinder."

"What's a cylinder?" asked Ed.

I clicked on CYLINDER.

"Flat round top,

flat round bottom,"

flashed on the computer.

"Here they are," said Ed.

He held up the two cylinders.

"No, here they are," said Ellie, "these have a

flat, round part, too."

"But they only have *one* side that's flat and

round," I said.

"They must be the cones. Don't they look like

ice cream cones?"

We attached a cone to one end of each cylinder.

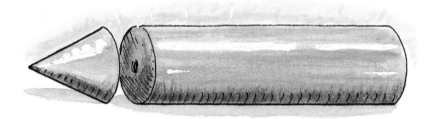

Then I clicked on STEP THREE.

"Find the square pyramid," I read from the computer screen.

"Hint: A square pyramid has four triangles and one square face.

Put in the batteries and you are almost done!"

"We are?" I asked.

We looked through the remaining pieces and found the square pyramid.

I popped in the batteries.

There was a quick flash.

I could have sworn something *winked* at me!

"What is it?" Ed asked.

"Something silly," said Ellie.

"Well, it's sure not a pen," I said.

Whoops! I just checked the time.

I'm late for baseball practice. G2G!

More to come tomorrow.

Your best friend,

Jan

Dear Nick,

I wish you still lived on Pine Street.
I wish you could have been here Saturday and
seen with your very own eyes the amazing,
fantastic, COOL thing that happened next.
Read on!

I clicked on STEP FOUR.
I watched these words
scroll down the computer screen.
"Attach everything to the big cube.
Congratulations! You have built the
INCREDIBLE TG 123!"
Not quite.

"What big cube?" I asked.

I clicked on CUBE.

"Six square faces,

12 edges,

eight corners,"

came up on the screen.

"Is that like a giant ice cube?" asked Ellie.

"Yes," I said. "But where is it?"

I didn't see a cube anywhere.

"How can we finish Grandma Ada's

birthday present? We don't have all the parts!"

Ed cried.

Things looked bad.

And they got worse!

I clicked on HELP.

The computer fizzled.

The screen went blank.

"Now what do we do?" I cried.

"I know what I'm going to do," said Ed.

"I'm going to make a birthday card for Grandma Ada."

"And I'm going to help Max blow up the balloons," said Ellie.

Everyone gave up—except me.

I pushed and pulled the blocks
this way and that.
I moved them up, over, and all around
each other.
I stared at the blocks and did some hard
thinking.
I wanted to build the Incredible TG 123
more than anything.
And guess what, Nick?
I did!
They don't call me JANCAN for nothing!
Can you figure out how I did it?

Your best friend,
Jan

P.S.: The INCREDIBLE TG 123

blew up 80 balloons in ten minutes,

danced with Grandma Ada,

and even fixed my computer

so I could send you these e-mails.

Come visit us soon. Come see it for yourself.

TG 123: it's incredible!

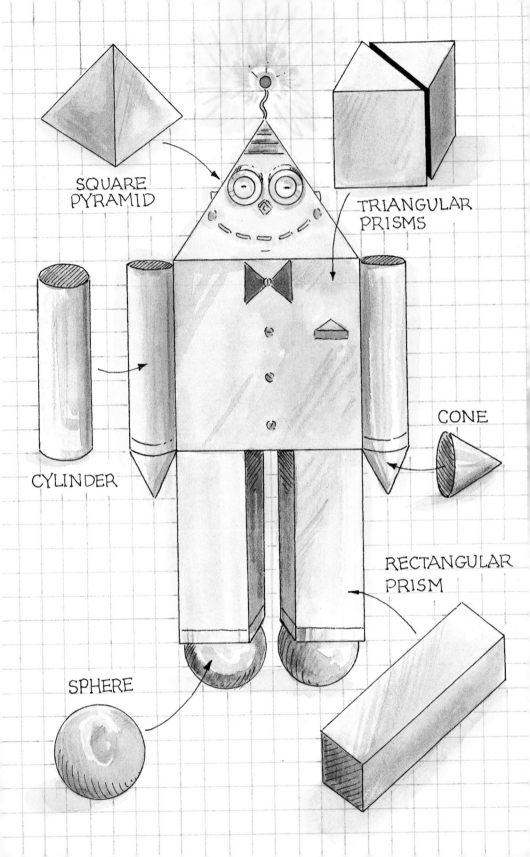

SQUARE PYRAMID

TRIANGULAR PRISMS

CYLINDER

CONE

RECTANGULAR PRISM

SPHERE

• ABOUT THE ACTIVITIES •

Learning about squares, circles, triangles, and other two-dimensional shapes is important, but working with three-dimensional materials provides a way for children to connect new math understanding to hands-on experiences.

Before they even come to school, young children discover from play experiences that the world is made up of different-sized and -shaped solids. When children play, they use blocks and other toys to create representations of many real-world situations. They build bridges, construct houses, and set up tea parties. Manipulating three-dimensional objects engages children in sorting, matching, fitting, combining, and comparing, all important skills that will help them learn about properties of space like shape, size, and position.

In school, children continue exploring and making discoveries with three-dimensional objects. They learn to examine their mathematical properties and begin to use standard terminology to describe geometric solids.

The Incredibly Awesome Box builds on children's experiences and curiosity and helps them connect appropriate mathematical language to geometric solids. Read the story with your child and then try the following activities. They're designed to help your child discover mathematical relationships in shapes that are all around us.

Enjoy the math!

—Marilyn Burns

You'll find tips and suggestions for guiding the activities whenever you see a box like this!

Retelling the Story

For Grandma Ada's birthday gift, Jan and her four cousins chipped in $5.00 each. Mom added $10.00. How much money did they have to spend? What did they decide to buy?

How did Jan and her cousins know, even before they opened the box, that the delivery people had dropped off the wrong gift?

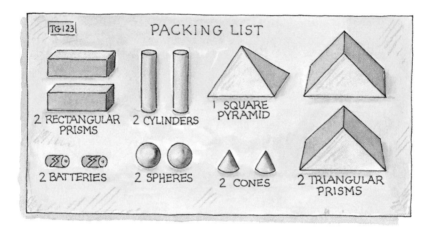

The packing list told them what shapes were in the box. How many shapes were there?

All of the shapes came in pairs except for one. Which was the shape that didn't have a match?

To put the blocks together, Jan and her cousins had to follow the computer directions. First they had to find two rectangular prisms and two spheres. How did they figure out which were these shapes?

Then they had to attach a cone to the end of each of the cylinders. How did they figure out which were these shapes?

Next they had to find a square pyramid. What hint did the computer screen give for finding this shape?

Finally, they had to attach everything to the big cube. But there was no big cube! What did Jan do?

Do you think Grandma Ada liked her gift? Would you like it?

Making Boxes

You can make a box by folding a piece of cardboard or heavy paper—if the paper is the right shape. Draw a T-shape like the one shown on the opposite page. Then cut it out, fold on the dotted lines, and tape it together.

When every side of a box is a square, the box is called a cube.

To make boxes that aren't cubes, try drawing, folding, and taping other shapes as shown.

What can you build using all your boxes?

Making a box from cardboard or paper is a way to help your child see relationships between two-dimensional and three-dimensional shapes. File folders are good to use for this activity. You probably will need to draw the flat shapes for your child, but encourage him or her to do as much of the cutting, folding, and taping as possible.

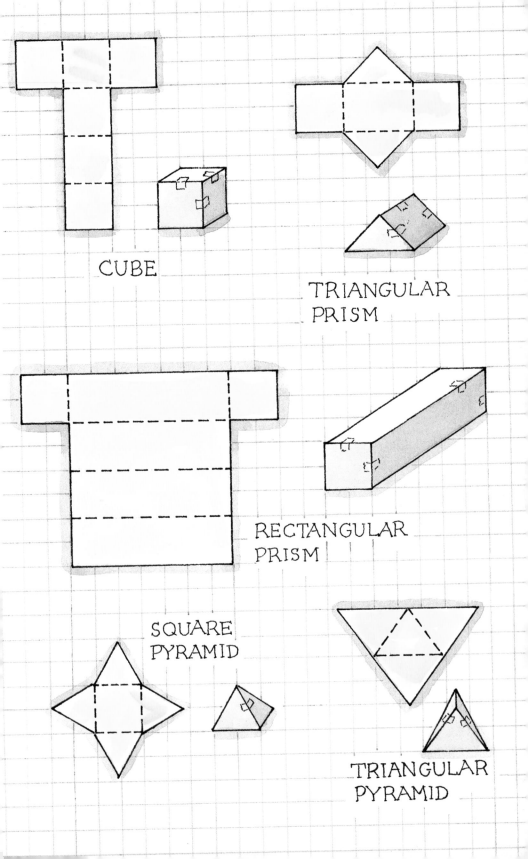

CUBE

TRIANGULAR
PRISM

RECTANGULAR
PRISM

SQUARE
PYRAMID

TRIANGULAR
PYRAMID

Shape Search

Jan and her cousins had to learn about the shapes that came in the box: the rectangular prism, the sphere, the cone, the cylinder, the square pyramid, the triangular prism, and the cube.

The stick of butter that Ed found was in the shape of a rectangular prism. Can you find examples of the other shapes? (For example, a ball is in the shape of a sphere.) Look around your home for boxes, containers, or toys of different shapes and match them with their names.

Same and Different

This is a game for two people. You each need a container from the cupboard, such as a large cereal box, a round salt box, or a small raisin box. Any size will do.

Take turns telling something that is the same about your containers. Keep going until you can't think of anything new. Then take turns telling something that is different about your containers. Keep going until you can't think of anything else.

Try the game with different containers.

Children will often focus on non-mathematical attributes of the containers. For example: They both have writing on them. They're both cardboard. One has red on it and the other doesn't. These observations are fine, but on your turn, try to point out mathematical attributes such as the number of faces, the number of corners, the shape of the faces, or the number of edges.